# MIGHTY PUP POWER!

By Hollis James
Based on the teleplay "Mighty Pups" by Andy Guerdat and Steve Sullivan
Illustrated by Fabrizio Petrossi

A GOLDEN BOOK • NEW YORK

T#: 593379

rhcbooks.com

ISBN 978-0-525-57772-0

Printed in the United States of America

10 9 8 7 6 5 4 3

It was a big day at Adventure Bay Beach because Mayor Humdinger was preparing to blast off in his rocket ship!

"Ladies and gentlemen," he announced, "I am about to become the very first mayor on the moon!" He whispered to his nephew, Harold, who was in charge of the launch, "Quick! I want to lift off before the PAW Patrol gets here and stops my foolproof plan!"

Just then, Harold accidentally launched the rocket!

"Excuse me—to be the first mayor on the moon, shouldn't I be *in* that rocket?" said Mayor Humdinger.

But the rocket wasn't going to the moon.

It was headed right for a meteor! The rocket bumped into the meteor and sent it straight down to Earth.

Meanwhile, Everest and Jake were stargazing. They saw the meteor coming toward Adventure Bay!

"Better call Ryder!" said Jake.

"Ryder, come in!" said Everest. "There's a meteor headed this way!"

"Uh-oh! We have to get everyone to safety," said Ryder.

Ryder split the pups into two groups. He led one group, and Chase headed the other. Chase hoped he would be a good leader.

"Attention, Adventure Bay!" said Chase through his bullhorn. "A meteor is headed toward us!"

The PAW Patrol cleared the streets just before the meteor crashed!

While investigating the meteorite, the PAW Patrol pups were zapped with a strange energy. Suddenly, they had superpowers!

Chase was super fast. Rubble was super strong. Skye could fly without wings. Everest could breathe ice, and Marshall could create amazing heat. Zuma's paws could shoot jets of water, and Rocky could make glowing super tools!

"Wow! I'm going to call you Mighty Pups!" said Ryder.

But it wasn't just the pups who had powers. Harold could make anything he wanted just by moving his hands! He made himself some rocket shoes and zoomed to Mayor Humdinger's lair.

"That meteorite can make me *Super* Mayor!" Mayor Humdinger snickered.

Harold used his mighty powers to build a super vehicle. They used it to take the meteorite from city hall.

Mayor Goodway quickly called the PAW Patrol.

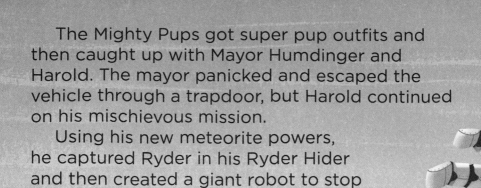

The Mighty Pups got super pup outfits and then caught up with Mayor Humdinger and Harold. The mayor panicked and escaped the vehicle through a trapdoor, but Harold continued on his mischievous mission.

Using his new meteorite powers, he captured Ryder in his Ryder Hider and then created a giant robot to stop the Mighty Pups.

Chase had to take the lead. "Zuma, make a mini lake in front of him. And, Everest, some ice would be nice!"

The robot slid on the icy lake—and totally wiped out!

But then the robot got back up.
"A little fall won't stop my pup-rounder-upper!"
said Harold. "Super rocket thrusters, coming up!"
The robot became rocket-powered!

Using its rockets, the robot quickly caught all the Mighty Pups—except Chase.

"What would Ryder do?" Chase asked himself. "Ryder says a good leader never gives up, so neither will I!"

"Mighty Pups, I have a plan!" said Chase. "Mighty Marshall, it's time to go *hot dog* on these nets!"

"Super idea, Team Leader Chase!" said Marshall as his paws began to glow red-hot. He melted the nets, freeing the pups.

Harold piloted his robot to go after Team Leader Chase.

"I've got you this time," said Harold. But his helmet fell down over his eyes. "Oops!"

The robot lurched to the Lookout and wrapped its arms and legs around it. Its rockets fired, and the Lookout took off—with Ryder trapped inside!

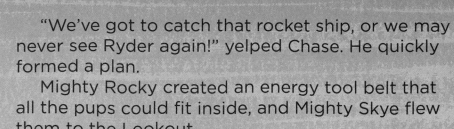

"We've got to catch that rocket ship, or we may never see Ryder again!" yelped Chase. He quickly formed a plan.

Mighty Rocky created an energy tool belt that all the pups could fit inside, and Mighty Skye flew them to the Lookout.

Inside the Lookout, Ryder knew the Mighty Pups had to get to the meteorite to stop the runaway robot. And he knew just how to help them!

The pups saw something shining on the robot's backpack.

"It's the PAW Patrol signal!" said Mighty Skye.

Chase knew what it meant. "It's Ryder!" he exclaimed. "He's showing us that the meteorite is in the robot's backpack!"

"Let's get that meteorite!" said Chase. "Rubble, can you reach it?"

"It might be a stretch," Rubble said, "but I'll give it a double-Rubble effort!"

The powerful pup swung up to the backpack and opened it with his Claw Arm. Then Mighty Rocky used his Super Vac to suck up the meteorite!

"Got it!" said Mighty Rocky.

Without the meteorite, the robot suddenly lost power and the Lookout began to fall. Chase needed a powerful whirlwind to slow it down.

"On it!" said Mighty Skye as she created super-strong spinning wind.

The wind slowed the Lookout, but it was still falling!

Chase used his super speed to make the whirlwind even stronger. He ran faster and faster until the Lookout finally slowed and landed . . . right where it belonged.

The meteorite stopped glowing. The robot had drained its energy, and the Mighty Pups lost their mighty powers. But they had saved the Lookout—and Ryder.

"You all did a great job, pups!" said Ryder. "Especially you, Team Leader Chase!"

"Thank you for saving Adventure Bay!" said Mayor Goodway.

"Whenever there's mighty trouble," said Ryder, "just yelp for help!"